THE
Terrible
TRICKSTER

ALSO BY FRANCES WATTS
AND ILLUSTRATED BY GREGORY ROGERS

The Secret of the Swords

The Poison Plot

Tournament Trouble

The Siege Scare

Pigeon Problems

SWORD GIRL

THE

Terrible

TRICKSTER

FRANCES WATTS

ILLUSTRATED BY **GREGORY ROGERS**

ALLEN&UNWIN

SYDNEY·MELBOURNE·AUCKLAND·LONDON

First published in 2013

Allen & Unwin
83 Alexander Street
Crows Nest NSW 2065
Australia
Phone: (61 2) 8425 0100
Fax: (61 2) 9906 2218
Email: info@allenandunwin.com
Web: www.allenandunwin.com

A Cataloguing-in-Publication entry is available from the National Library
of Australia
www.trove.nla.gov.au

ISBN 978 1 74331 321 3

Cover design by Seymour Designs
Cover illustration by Gregory Rogers
Text design by Seymour Designs
Set in 16/21 pt Adobe Jenson Pro by Seymour Designs
This book was printed in July 2014 at Griffin Press,
168 Cross Keys Road, Salisbury South SA 5016.

10 9 8 7 6 5 4 3 2

MIX
Paper from
responsible sources
FSC
www.fsc.org   FSC® C009448

The paper in this book is FSC® certified.
FSC® promotes environmentally responsible,
socially beneficial and economically viable
management of the world's forests.

For ma chère tante, *Anne-Marie*

F. W.

For Matt

G. R.

CHAPTER 1

Clip-clop, clip-clop, clip-clop.

Tommy woke to the sound of a horse's hooves on the flagstones of Flamant Castle's great courtyard.

She sprang out of bed, worried that she must have slept in, but there was no light coming through the small window set high in the thick stone wall. Puzzled, Tommy climbed back into bed.

Who could be arriving in the dead of the night? It must be a messenger, she thought. And the message must be urgent for him to arrive at this hour. The castle's sentries would never have lowered the drawbridge otherwise.

She listened for signs of activity in the courtyard below. A groom would be fetched to lead the messenger's horse to the stables, and a page would be sent for to take the messenger to Sir Benedict, the castle's bravest knight. If the news was very serious, maybe even Sir Walter the Bald, the nobleman who owned the castle, would be woken.

All was quiet, however, except for a soft, 'Woah there,' followed by the *clip-clop* of hooves heading in the direction of the stables.

Tommy lay awake, wondering about what she had just heard. Where had the messenger come from? And why had no one come to greet him? The questions

chased round and round in her mind until at last she fell into an uneasy sleep.

The next thing she knew, sun was streaming in through the little window. Down below she could hear carts clattering across the flagstones of the courtyard as the local merchants made their deliveries to the kitchen.

Oh no! She'd slept in!

Tommy leaped out of bed and pulled on her tunic and leggings. She didn't want to be late for her work in the armoury. Since becoming Flamant Castle's Keeper of the Blades, Tommy looked after all the bladed weapons. It was a very important job, as the knights who defended the castle relied on her to keep their swords sharpened and polished. If she did her job well, Tommy hoped that she might become a squire and train to be a knight herself.

'Good morning, Mrs Moon,' Tommy said as she entered the kitchen. Even though she wasn't a kitchen girl anymore, she still took her meals at the long table where she used to peel potatoes, dreaming that one day she would be holding a sword instead of a paring knife.

'Good morning, Thomasina,' the cook replied. She cut a slice of bread from a giant loaf. 'You'll catch flies in there if you're not careful,' she observed as Tommy opened her mouth wide in a yawn.

'Excuse me,' said Tommy, covering her mouth. 'I woke up in the middle of the night when that messenger arrived. He must have had important news.'

'A messenger in the middle of the night?' Mrs Moon sounded doubtful. 'Perhaps you dreamed it.'

When she had finished her bread and a glass of milk, Tommy hurried across the courtyard towards the armoury. Was it possible that she had dreamed the sound of a horse's hooves? As if in answer to her question, a shrill neigh rang out, followed by another, then another. It sounded as if all the castle's horses were in distress!

Tommy immediately ran towards the archway that would take her to the stables. She had to see if Bess was all right.

Although Bess was Sir Benedict's horse, Tommy had been allowed to ride her regularly ever since they had competed together in a tournament.

The small courtyard outside the stables was full of horses, all looking cross. Grooms and stable boys were trying to calm them. She found Bess stamping around near the water trough.

'Are you all right?' Tommy asked the chestnut mare. 'I could hear neighing from the great courtyard.'

'It's that bay stallion who arrived last night,' Bess grumbled. 'He's a cheeky rascal. Ever since he got here he's been nothing but trouble, nipping and wanting to play, stealing other horses' hay. He just won't leave us in peace. We've had enough.'

'It must be the horse of the messenger I heard in the night,' said Tommy. 'I'll talk to the stable master about him. Maybe he can be stabled somewhere else so that he doesn't disturb the castle's horses.'

Tommy found the tall, wiry stable master in the far corner of the yard. He was talking to Sir Benedict.

'I don't know what's got into them,' the stable master was saying. 'They all just went berserk.'

'Excuse me, sir,' Tommy spoke up. 'It's the bay stallion that's the problem. The messenger's horse.'

Both men turned to look at Tommy, clearly surprised to see her.

'Shouldn't you be in the armoury, Tommy?' the knight asked.

'Yes, Sir Benedict. I was on my way there when I heard the horses. I wanted to make sure Bess was all right.'

'She's fine,' said the stable master. 'Not as highly strung as some of the others.' He tilted his head in the direction of a black gelding who was bucking and kicking in the centre of a circle of stable hands. 'But what's this about a bay stallion? There's no bay stallion in the stables.'

'It's the messenger's horse,' Tommy repeated. 'The one who arrived last night.'

The stable master looked at Sir Benedict questioningly.

The knight shook his head. 'I'm not sure what you mean, Tommy. No messenger arrived in the night. I spoke to the sentries myself not ten minutes ago and they would have reported the arrival of a stranger.'

'Oh.' Tommy blinked. 'I'm sorry. I – I must have made a mistake.'

Embarrassed, Tommy walked back through the archway to the great courtyard. So Mrs Moon had been right. There had been no horse and rider in the night; it was all a dream.

Then she stopped. But if it was only a dream, what about the bay stallion Bess had mentioned?

CHAPTER 2

WHEN TOMMY ENTERED the armoury the air was ringing with the sound of a hammer beating metal. The blacksmith looked up from the shield he was working on.

'You're late this morning, Sword Girl,' he said. 'That's not like you.'

'I'm sorry, Smith,' Tommy said. 'I stopped at the stables on my way here. Something's got into the horses and they're all upset.'

'They probably got a look at your ugly face.' Reynard, the Keeper of the Bows, was lounging in the doorway of the bow chamber. He had hated Tommy ever since Sir Benedict had made her the Keeper of the Blades, a position Reynard had wanted for himself.

Ignoring him, Tommy went into the sword chamber. Swords stood in racks lining three sides of the narrow room, the light from the candle on the wall reflected in their gleaming blades. On her bench lay half a dozen swords that she had sharpened the day before using a file and whetstone. Now she picked up her cloth and a pot of clove-scented oil and set about polishing them.

'You're running late this morning, Sword Girl,' said a disapproving voice. 'I hope you're not growing neglectful of your duties.'

Tommy turned to face the small rack of swords in the darkest corner of the chamber. None of the knights or squires ever used these swords, which were known

as the Old Wrecks. But since she had
become the Keeper of the Blades Tommy
had learned that the Old Wrecks were
inhabited by the spirits of their previous
owners. The voice had come from Bevan
Brumm, a long-handled dagger who had
been a merchant.

'Neglectful? Our sword girl?' scoffed a sabre. This was Nursie, who had been Sir Walter's nursemaid when he was a boy. 'Why, the very idea! *We* were the neglected ones until she came along.'

'I heard a lot of noise coming from the stables,' Tommy explained, 'and I went to see what was wrong.'

'And did you find out?' asked a slender sword with a curved blade. Jasper Swann, a squire, had fallen ill and died when he was close to Tommy's own age; perhaps that was why he often seemed to understand how Tommy was feeling.

'Not exactly,' said Tommy. 'I was woken in the night by a horse and rider in the courtyard – at least, I thought I was, but Sir Benedict said no one came to the castle last night. So I must have dreamed it. Yet when I talked to Bess in the stables she said that a strange horse had arrived in the night. So I can't have dreamed it.' She shook her head in confusion.

'That's very mysterious,' said Jasper. 'What do you think is going on?'

Tommy sighed. 'I have no idea,' she said. 'But I know who to ask. I'll go and find her when I've finished my work here.'

Many hours had passed by the time Tommy replaced the last sword in the rack and walked out into the courtyard. The light seemed bright after the gloom of the sword chamber, though the sun was low over the battlements.

She looked around the courtyard for the black and white cat who could often be found dozing on a sun-warmed flagstone. Lil always knew everything that was happening around the castle. Perhaps she would be able to solve the mystery of the horse and rider.

But Lil was nowhere to be seen, so Tommy ran through the castle gate and down the grassy bank to the moat. There she found the cat, asleep on the grass at the water's edge, while her friend the crocodiddle backstroked up and down in front of her.

Tommy sat down beside the cat.

'Hello, Sword Girl,' called the crocodiddle. He flipped over and paddled towards her.

'Hi, Mr Crocodiddle,' Tommy replied.

Lil opened her eyes, stretched and yawned, which made Tommy yawn too.

'You look tired, Tommy,' the cat commented.

'That's because I was woken in the night,' Tommy told her. 'I thought I heard a messenger arriving, but the sentries didn't see anybody. Then Bess told me there is a strange horse in the stables, though the stable master doesn't know anything about it.'

'Curious,' said the cat, looking alert now.

'The horse and rider in the middle of the night?' The crocodiddle rested his long snout on the bank. 'That wasn't a messenger. It was the red-headed boy.'

'Red-headed boy?' Tommy said in surprise. 'You mean Reynard?'

The crocodiddle slapped the water with his tail. 'That's him – the nasty one.'

'Well that explains why the sentries didn't report it: he's not a stranger to the castle. But why would Reynard bring a horse into the castle in the middle of the night? What is he up to?' Tommy and Lil looked at each other, mystified, but neither had an answer.

As she ran back through the castle gate on her way to the kitchen for dinner, Tommy kept turning the question over and over in her mind: what was Reynard up to? She knew one thing for sure: he'd be up to no good.

CHAPTER 3

THE AROMA OF HEARTY vegetable soup filled the kitchen as Tommy slipped through the door and took a seat at the long scrubbed table.

The cook was ladling soup into bowls that were arranged on enormous trays. When the bowls were full, the trays were carried by serving girls to the banqueting hall, where Sir Walter and the knights

waited for their dinner.

'It smells delicious, Mrs Moon,' Tommy said when at last the cook placed a steaming bowl in front of her. She dipped her spoon into the soup and took a big mouthful – and immediately spat it out.

'Thomasina!'

'I'm sorry, Mrs Moon, but it ... it tastes terrible!'

'Don't be ridiculous, girl. You've had my vegetable soup a hundred times.' Mrs Moon lowered a ladle into the cauldron then sipped from it. Her face screwed up in disgust. 'My stars! Something's wrong with the soup.' The cook sounded

bewildered. 'But I made it just the way I always do.'

At that moment one of the girls who had been serving the knights ran in. 'Mrs Moon, the knights are all spitting out their soup!'

The cook put a hand to her mouth. 'Oh no, the knights! What if my soup makes them ill?' Looking determined, she took another sip of the awful brew. Then her lips tightened into a thin line. 'I know what's happened here. Someone has put sugar in my salt cellar!'

Mrs Moon turned to the serving girl. 'Run back to the banqueting hall and tell the other girls to remove the soup bowls at once. We'll have to serve the meat course straight away.'

She took off her apron and handed it to Tommy. 'I know you don't work in the kitchen anymore, Thomasina, but this is an emergency. I need you to help get that soup back.'

'Of course, Mrs Moon.'

Tommy tied on the apron, picked up an empty tray and hurried after the serving girl.

The banqueting hall was loud with the voices of the knights who were crowded around long wooden tables.

Tommy was placing bowls on her tray when she heard a familiar voice say, 'What on earth has got into Mrs Moon, Tommy? That soup was as sweet as custard!' It was Sir Benedict.

'It wasn't Mrs Moon's fault, sir,' Tommy said. 'Someone put sugar in her salt cellar.' She couldn't stop a small giggle escaping as she pictured the knights spitting out their sweet soup.

The knight frowned. 'Well I think it was a silly trick.'

Tommy tried to look serious. 'Yes, sir.' She picked up Sir Benedict's soup bowl and put it on her tray.

The rest of the evening passed in a blur as Tommy, already tired from a hard day working in the sword

27

chamber, hurried back and forth between the kitchen and the banqueting hall with platters of roast boar and jugged hare, fried fish and eels in cream sauce.

It wasn't until she climbed the stairs to her sleeping quarters that Tommy realised she hadn't had any dinner herself. But she was so exhausted she didn't care. She fell asleep as soon as her head touched the pillow, and if a strange rider – or Reynard – arrived on a horse in the middle of the night, Tommy didn't hear him.

Tommy woke early the next morning, determined not to be late for work again. She was crossing the great courtyard on the way to the armoury when she was startled by a shrill cry. Breaking into a run, she followed the noise into the small cobbled square outside the castle's laundry. There, one of the girls who worked in the laundry was pointing at a washtub and shrieking.

'What is it?' Tommy asked.

'Look at my white sheets!' The girl lifted a sheet from the tub and Tommy saw that it was bright yellow.

Before Tommy could ask what had happened, the castle's small, round physician entered the square at a run, his brown robes flapping behind him.

'Is someone hurt?' the physician asked. 'I heard a scream.'

In answer, the laundry girl held up the yellow sheet. 'I left it soaking overnight – and now look. It's meant to be white!'

'Oh dear,' said the physician. He bent over to inspect the water in the tub, then fished out a soggy mass of dried leaves. 'This is weld,' he said. 'Its leaves are used as a yellow dye. I'm afraid someone's played a trick on you.'

'But the sheets …' said the girl. 'How can I make them white again?'

The physician shook his head. 'I'm afraid there's no cure for yellow sheets.'

'You mean they're ruined?' the girl wailed. 'I'm going to be in so much trouble.' She began to weep.

'What's going on here?'

Tommy turned at the sound of Sir Benedict's voice.

'Tommy?' the knight said. 'Why aren't you in the armoury?'

'Someone's played a trick and turned the sheets yellow,' she explained.

'Another trick?' Sir Benedict didn't sound

amused. 'Tommy, don't you have work to do in the sword chamber?'

'Yes, Sir Benedict,' she murmured. As she walked away, she wondered who had played the trick on the laundry girl. Could it be the same person who had put sugar in Mrs Moon's salt cellar?

'Ah, there you are, Sword Girl,' Smith said as Tommy entered the armoury. 'We were starting to worry about you, weren't we, Reynard?'

Reynard was standing next to the forge, his face smug. 'Sir Walter was looking for you,' he said. 'He wanted his sword sharpened and polished.'

'Oh no!' said Tommy. 'I'll do it straight away.'

'There's no need,' said Reynard. 'Since

you weren't here, I took care of Sir Walter's sword for him. He was very grateful. Maybe he'll make *me* Keeper of the Blades instead of you.'

Tommy stared at him, open-mouthed. Would Sir Walter really do that? She probably deserved it, she told herself with a heavy heart. She should have been there to help Sir Walter.

Walking into the sword chamber, she let out a groan. Reynard might have done a good job of polishing Sir Walter's sword, but he'd left her tools and equipment scattered all over the floor.

'Late again, Sword Girl,' Bevan Brumm remarked. 'It's becoming quite a habit.'

'Where on earth have you been?' Nursie chimed in. 'Sir Walter was here and that horrible Keeper of the Bows had to help him with his sword.'

'I'm late because of a trick,' Tommy explained.

'Someone put some dye into a washtub at the laundry and it turned all the sheets yellow. I heard a laundry girl scream and I went to see what was the matter.'

'The poor lass,' said Nursie sympathetically.

'And that's not the only trick,' Tommy said. 'Last night, someone replaced the salt in Mrs Moon's salt cellar with sugar, and ruined the soup.'

As Tommy described how the knights had all spat out their soup, Jasper Swann smothered a laugh.

'A trick like that is no laughing matter, Jasper Swann,' Bevan Brumm scolded.

'Dearie me,' said Nursie. 'It sounds like we have a trickster at the castle. You mark my words, it'll turn life at Flamant upside down.'

CHAPTER 4

Despite Nursie's prediction, the day passed just like any other day. Tommy was kept busy sharpening the swords of some knights who were going out on patrol the next morning, and it was dark by the time she crossed the great courtyard to the kitchen.

A bowl of bean and barley soup was cooling on the table as Tommy slipped

into her seat. She was just
about to lift the spoon
to her lips when the
serving girl from the
night before burst into
the kitchen. She was
panting as if she had run all the way from
the banqueting hall.

'Mrs Moon! Mrs Moon!' the girl
exclaimed.

'What is it, girl?' the cook demanded.

'The knights … the soup …'

'There's nothing wrong with the soup,'
Mrs Moon said. 'I tasted it myself.'

'You'd better come see,' the girl said.
If Tommy didn't know better, she'd
have thought the girl was on the verge of
giggling.

'Hmph.' Mrs Moon untied her apron and hurried after the girl. Tommy, curious, followed them.

Even before they reached the banqueting hall, Tommy could tell something was wrong. Instead of the normal babble of voices and laughter echoing from the high stone walls of the hall, all Tommy could hear was ... sneezes?

When she stepped inside, she saw that

all the knights were sneezing and sniffing. Some were wiping their streaming eyes while others honked into handkerchiefs.

'My stars!' the cook gasped. 'What in heaven's name is going on here?'

'I don't know,' the serving girl said. 'It started when they reached for the salt cellars.'

A knight nearby said, 'Someone has changed the salt – *ah-CHOO!* – for sneezing powder.'

Mrs Moon's eyes grew wide. 'Another trick with the salt?' With Tommy close behind, the cook weaved her way through the tables to where Sir Benedict was sitting. His nose and eyes were red from sneezing.

'Good evening, Mrs Moon,' he wheezed. 'And Tommy – what are you doing here?

It seems you're to be found everywhere but the sword chamber these days.'

Tommy ducked her head. Had Sir Walter told Sir Benedict that Tommy wasn't in the sword chamber that morning?

'Sir Benedict,' Mrs Moon said, 'I've just heard about the sneezing powder in the salt and I can assure you that this trick has nothing to do with my kitchen. I checked the salt cellar myself.'

'Don't worry, Mrs Moon,' said Sir Benedict. 'I know – *ah-CHOO!* – that you're not to blame. You can go back to the kitchen.' When the cook had gone, the knight continued, 'Someone's been having a little fun with us, it appears. Someone who has been popping up wherever there's a commotion, whether it's in the stables or the kitchen or the laundry or the banqueting hall.' He looked at Tommy. 'These tricks might seem funny, but there's no room for them at Flamant Castle. Tricksters are not welcome here.'

Tommy's heart almost stopped as she realised why Sir Benedict was looking at her so sternly. He thought that she was the trickster!

CHAPTER 5

'But Sir Benedict—' Tommy began.

The knight held up his hand. Sir Walter had risen from his seat and was about to speak.

'Ah-CHOO!' said the nobleman. He blew his nose into a large pink and blue handkerchief embroidered with a flamingo, just like the one on the Flamant Castle crest. 'All this sneezing has wrecked my appetite,' he declared. 'I'm going to bed. Goodnight all.'

The knights rose and ducked their heads respectfully.

'Goodnight, Sir Walter,' they chorused.

When the nobleman had left the banqueting hall, Sir Benedict turned to

Tommy once more. 'We'll speak about this again in the morning, Tommy,' he told her. 'You should probably go to bed now. When I see Smith tomorrow I expect him to tell me that you were at work in the sword chamber bright and early.'

'Yes, Sir Benedict,' Tommy whispered, finding it hard to speak over the lump in her throat.

When she stepped into the great courtyard, she saw Lil sitting on a low wall.

Tommy sat down beside her friend. 'Someone put sneezing powder in the salt cellars in the banqueting hall,' she said.

The cat started to laugh. 'That must have been quite a sight – a hall full of knights all sneezing at once.'

'I suppose so,' said Tommy.

'Tommy?' The cat turned to her. 'You look miserable. What's wrong?'

'Sir Benedict thinks it was me!' Tommy cried. 'He thinks that I put the sugar in Mrs Moon's salt cellar, and made the laundry girl's sheets turn yellow, and changed the knights' salt for sneezing powder! He thinks that I'm the trickster!'

'Sir Benedict thinks you're the trickster?' Lil shook her head. 'Surely not.'

'He says every time there's a trick played I'm there, and he's right – but it wasn't me! I wouldn't! You believe me, don't you, Lil?'

'Of course I do,' said the cat firmly. 'Don't you worry, Tommy. We'll prove you're not to blame.'

'But how?' said Tommy.

'Simple,' said the cat. 'We'll find out who

the real trickster is.' There was a determined glint in her green eyes.

'Do you really think—' Tommy started, but at that moment the peace of the courtyard was shattered by a roar.

'What was that?' Tommy gasped.

She and Lil watched in astonishment as Sir Walter raced into the courtyard in his nightgown and cap. He ran to the well, pulled up a bucket and emptied it over his head.

As he stood dripping on the flagstones, he let out a giant sneeze.

This was followed by a swell of voices as the knights began to pour out of the banqueting hall to see what had caused the roar.

Tommy stood up. 'I'd better get up to bed before Sir Benedict sees me out here and thinks that I did something to harm Sir Walter. Goodnight, Lil.'

The next morning Tommy was feeling gloomy as she walked across the great courtyard to the armoury. How could Sir Benedict think that she would play those tricks? She remembered what he had said: *These tricks might seem funny, but there's no*

room for them at Flamant Castle. Tricksters are not welcome here. Lil was right: they had to find out who the real trickster was – or Tommy could be sent away from the castle!

Reynard would get his wish then, she thought angrily. He would probably be made the Keeper of the Blades, just like he'd always wanted. Suddenly, it occurred to her that while she was getting the blame for the tricks, Reynard had been unusually helpful in the armoury. While she had been delayed by the laundry trick, he was taking care of Sir Walter's sword. And the day before, she had been late because of the ruckus in the stables – and that ruckus had been caused by Reynard's horse! The more she considered it, the more she thought that Reynard must be behind all the tricks.

She was already at work in the sword chamber when she heard Reynard enter the armoury.

'Did you hear about Sir Walter?' he said to Smith. 'Someone put itching powder in his sheets! What a great trick!'

'I don't think Sir Walter would agree with you, lad,' Smith replied.

'That's because he doesn't have a good sense of humour like me,' Reynard boasted. 'I think it's the best trick ever.'

Aha! Now Tommy was sure that Reynard was the culprit.

She waited until she could hear Smith hammering away at a dented shield, then marched into the bow chamber.

Reynard was using his slingshot to fire pebbles at a crossbow mounted on the wall.

'I know you're the trickster, so you'd better watch out,' Tommy warned. 'I'm going to tell Sir Benedict it was you and he's going to send you away from the castle.'

If Reynard was worried by her threat he didn't show it. 'So you think I'm the

trickster, do you?' he said. 'I bet you don't have any proof, Sword Girl.'

Tommy hesitated. Then she remembered the horse making trouble in the stables. The crocodiddle had seen Reynard ride into the castle on that horse.

'Yes I do!' she said triumphantly. 'There's the bay stallion.'

'The bay stallion?' Reynard sounded surprised.

'You thought no one knew about that, didn't you?' Tommy said. 'But I do, and so will Sir Benedict.' And with that, she left the room.

Back in the sword chamber, Tommy concentrated on her work. One of Sir Walter's pages had brought the nobleman's sword back. Holding it by the ruby-studded

hilt, she took extra care about polishing the steel blade, which was beautifully engraved with flamingos. The hours crept by as she waited for Sir Benedict to appear in the doorway of the sword chamber. *We'll speak about this again in the morning,* he had said. But the morning passed with no sign of the knight.

By afternoon, her courage was beginning to desert her. Even though Reynard had brought the troublesome horse to the castle, she had no proof that he had played the other tricks. It was just like Sir Benedict had said: the only person who had been present when all the tricks were played was Tommy herself. Even if she told him the trickster was Reynard, why should he believe her? He would just think less of her for trying to blame someone else. With a sigh, she turned her attention to the small rack in the corner.

'Is something wrong, Sword Girl?' Jasper Swann asked, quick to sense her mood as always.

'Yes, what is it, dearie?' Nursie wanted to know. 'You've been sighing away all day.'

Tommy picked up the long-handled dagger that was Bevan Brumm. 'It's Sir Benedict,' she confided as she rubbed oil into the blade. 'He thinks that I'm the trickster – and I'm scared he's going to send me away!'

CHAPTER 6

'SEND YOU AWAY from the castle?' Bevan Brumm said, shocked. 'You might have been neglecting your duties recently, but that is no reason to send you away.'

'She hasn't been neglecting her duties!' Jasper Swann protested. 'Both times she was late she had good reason.'

'And our sword girl is no trickster,' Nursie added loyally. 'She's much too kind to play cruel tricks. No one who knows you could believe such a thing.'

'Thank you, Nursie,' said Tommy.

'Who are you talking to?'

Tommy looked up to see a page standing in the doorway.

'Um … nobody,' she said. She replaced Bevan Brumm in the rack and rose from her stool. 'Can I help you?'

'Sir Benedict wants to see you in the great hall.'

'In the great hall?' Tommy repeated. She felt a fluttering in her stomach as she said the words. Whenever Sir Benedict had wanted to speak to her in the past, he had come to find her in the sword chamber. The great hall was used only for important occasions, like welcoming noblemen from other castles or planning battles or celebrating victories – or punishing wrongdoers.

Tommy's heart sank. It seemed her worst fears were coming true. Sir Benedict must be planning to send her away from Flamant.

She looked around the sword chamber. She had been happier in this small room than she had been in her whole life – learning all about swords, and learning the skills she would need if she was to her fulfil her dream of becoming a knight. And best of all were the friends she'd made since she became Keeper of the Blades. She gazed at the small rack that held the Old Wrecks. Would she be allowed to return to the sword chamber to say goodbye? she wondered.

Smith clearly had no idea of the fate that awaited her, for when Tommy said she was going to the great hall to see Sir Benedict he replied, 'If you see Reynard tell him I need him to fetch me some more tacks from the blacksmith in town.' He held up a shield with a broken strap. 'Sir Benedict has been flinging his shield around again.'

Tommy didn't know where Reynard had gone, and she didn't really care. It was his fault that she was being sent away from the castle. Her eyes pricked with tears at the unfairness of it.

Tommy followed the page across the courtyard and into the cloister leading to the great hall. The cloister was a long passageway with a high roof and beautifully carved windows that looked out onto the great courtyard. Glancing through one, Tommy saw Lil.

'Don't worry, Tommy,' the cat murmured. 'You'll be all right.'

Tommy felt tears prick again at the thought of leaving Lil. The cat was the best friend she had ever had. 'Thanks, Lil,' she whispered.

'Wait here,' the page instructed as they stepped into the great hall.

Tommy stopped, awestruck. She had passed through the hall once or twice, running errands, but she had never looked at it properly. Now, with light streaming through its high windows, which were carved in the shape of roses, she saw how magnificent it was. No wonder it was kept for special occasions.

To begin with, it was huge, the biggest room Tommy had ever seen – bigger even than the banqueting hall – and the vaulted ceiling soared almost as high as one of the castle's towers. The wall nearest to her was lined with a wall hanging, and banners decorated with the crest of Flamant Castle hung from the ceiling. Around the walls

were giant candelabras that stood taller than Tommy, with flickering candles that made the stone glow a rich honey colour.

She could see Sir Benedict at the far end of the hall, sitting at a table. Sir Hugh sat on one side of him and another knight, Sir Matthew, on the other. They looked serious. In front of them, with his back to her, stood Reynard. Tommy felt a bubble of anger rise in her: they were probably telling Reynard that he was the new Keeper of the Blades!

Suddenly aware that she was staring, Tommy quickly turned her head and fixed her gaze on the wall hanging beside her. Studying it, she saw that it told a story. On one section was stitched a castle she recognised as Flamant, with a hundred or more knights on horses galloping away across the fields. Tommy stepped quietly along to the next scene, in which the knights of Flamant were fighting a battle, their swords raised.

Her eye was drawn to a short, stout, red-haired knight carrying a Flamant shield. He looked familiar, she thought. But there was something funny about him, something not quite right ... When Tommy realised what it was, she almost exclaimed aloud. The red-haired knight was riding a blue horse!

She looked around for the page, to ask if he knew anything about the red-headed knight with the blue horse, but instead she saw Reynard.

The Keeper of the Bows was walking

towards her, his expression like thunder. 'This is your fault, Sword Girl,' he said angrily. 'You told Sir Benedict that I'd been playing tricks, didn't you?'

'What? No!' said Tommy.

'Now I'm being sent home.' His voice quavered. For a horrible moment, Tommy thought Reynard was going to burst into tears. 'And I didn't do anything!' He sounded so unhappy that Tommy almost believed him. After everything he'd done, she actually felt sorry for Reynard!

'But how did they know it was you?' she asked.

Before Reynard could respond, she heard

Sir Benedict call her name. 'Tommy? We're ready for you now.'

She walked the length of the great hall, feeling very small in the enormous space, until at last she reached the long table. Her heart was pounding as she stood before the three knights, dreading what they were about to say. If they knew Reynard was the trickster, why had they summoned her? Did they think she had been helping him?

'We have some bad news, Tommy,' Sir Benedict began.

'Yes, sir?' Tommy said, her heart hammering so loudly now she was sure the knights must hear it.

'I'm afraid we've had to ask Reynard to leave the castle. It turns out he was our trickster – not you.'

The relief that washed over Tommy was so great her legs trembled beneath her.

'How did you find out, sir?' she asked.

'A witness saw him,' Sir Hugh explained.

'In Sir Walter's own bedchamber!' exclaimed Sir Matthew.

'I'm truly sorry, Tommy,' said Sir Benedict. 'I should have known you were not a trickster, and I was wrong to accuse you. Will you accept my apology?'

Tommy was so overcome she couldn't speak, so she just nodded.

'But Reynard's leaving will mean extra work for you,' Sir Benedict continued. 'We'll need you to take over his duties as well as your own until we find a new Keeper of the Bows.'

'Of course, sir,' Tommy said. She didn't care if she had to work day and night if it meant she got to stay at the castle!

CHAPTER 7

Out in the great courtyard, Lil was waiting.

Tommy ran to her. 'Lil! I haven't been sent away after all! Sir Benedict knows that Reynard was the trickster.'

The cat smiled. 'That's wonderful, Tommy.' She didn't sound at all surprised.

'You already knew, didn't you?' Tommy said. 'How?'

Lil licked a paw and dabbed her whiskers with it. 'After the trick with the itching powder last night, I asked around – and I found someone who'd seen Reynard in Sir Walter's bedchamber. So of course we went straight to Sir Benedict.'

'Really?' Tommy said, thinking how lucky it was that, like her, Sir Benedict was able to talk with the castle's animals. 'Who saw him?'

In answer, Lil raised her head and called, 'Pigeon?'

At first nothing happened, and then a bird came to land on the flagstone beside them in a flurry of grey feathers.

His eyes darted from left to right. 'The physician's not around, is he?' The physician regularly asked the pigeon for droppings to

make his cures, but the pigeon – who was
a highly skilled message carrier – found it
insulting.

'I haven't seen him,' Tommy assured him.

'And you're not after any droppings
yourself?' the pigeon asked suspiciously.

Tommy blushed, because one time she
had asked the pigeon for his droppings,

when she wanted to make a cure for the crocodiddle's sneezles. 'No,' she said.

'Tommy was asking about what happened in Sir Walter's bedchamber,' Lil explained.

'Oh yes. Well, as I told Sir Benedict, I happened to be sitting on Sir Walter's windowsill last night waiting for him to return from dinner. Sometimes he likes me to coo him to sleep, you know. So I was just sitting there, humming some of Sir Walter's favourite lullabies, when I saw that nasty boy, the one with red hair.'

'Reynard?' said Tommy.

'Yes, that's him. Whenever he sees me he threatens to turn me into pigeon pie. Horrible boy.'

'And he was in Sir Walter's bedchamber?' Lil prompted patiently.

'Yes he was,' said the pigeon. 'He pulled back Sir Walter's blankets and then he took a pouch from his pocket and sprinkled a powder all over the sheets.'

'Itching powder,' breathed Tommy.

'Indeed,' said the pigeon. 'And the oaf was laughing and laughing as he left the room. Sir Benedict didn't like it when I told him that.'

'No,' Lil agreed. 'He didn't.'

'Ah, Sword Girl,' said Smith when Tommy returned to the armoury. 'I had a message from Sir Benedict saying that young Reynard's been sent away. So he was the trickster, eh?' He clicked his tongue against his teeth. 'It's like I told him: there's nothing funny at all about itching powder.'

'No, Smith,' said Tommy.

'And you're to look after blades *and* bows, then, are you? You'll have your work cut out for you and no mistake. Well you'd best run off to town and get them tacks for me, Sword Girl. Sir Benedict's shield won't mend itself.'

'I'll be as quick as I can,' Tommy promised.

''Course, he'll only go breaking the strap again in a day or two,' Smith was grumbling to himself as she ran out the door.

Tommy flew across the courtyard, determined to get to town and back in double-quick time. After all, she now had Reynard's work to do as well as her own.

She was crossing the bridge when she

heard a voice calling her from below. 'Sword Girl? Hey, Sword Girl!'

Tommy ran to the edge of the bridge and peered down at the moat. 'Hi, Mr Crocodiddle.'

'Where are you off to in such a hurry?'

'Smith needs some tacks from town.'

'Oh. I saw that red-haired boy walking towards town not long ago, but he didn't seem to be in a hurry.'

'Reynard's been sent home,' Tommy explained. 'He was playing tricks.'

'Ah, that explains why he was carrying a sack over his shoulder. I'd have thought he'd be riding his horse, though.'

'Hmm, that is strange,' said Tommy. 'I wonder why he'd leave his horse behind?'

She thought about this all the way to town, where she fetched the tacks from the blacksmith, and all the way back, but it still didn't make any sense.

'Where have you been?' asked Jasper Swann as soon as Tommy entered the sword chamber. 'What happened with Sir Benedict?'

Tommy told the Old Wrecks everything that had occurred since the page had summoned her to the great hall, finishing with: 'But I still don't understand why Reynard would leave his horse behind.' This reminded her of another mystery concerning horses.

'While I was waiting in the great hall,' she said, 'I saw this wall hanging.'

'I know the one,' said Nursie. 'It tells the story of the Battle of Barlow. My little darling used to love to look at it when he was a wee thing.' Nursie always referred to Sir Walter as her little darling.

'There was a knight from Flamant with red hair,' Tommy said. 'He looked familiar.'

'That would be Sir Ferdinand Foxe,' said Nursie. 'Or Sir Ferdy, as everyone called him. Of course, he was already an old man by the time I arrived at the castle as a young girl. Sir Ferdy fought alongside Sir Cyril, who was Sir Walter's grandfather.'

'The thing is,' said Tommy, 'in the wall hanging it looked like he was riding a blue horse.'

'Oh, he was a terrible trickster was Ferdy.' Tommy could tell Nursie didn't approve. 'Even in the middle of a battle he just couldn't be serious.'

'But where did he get a blue horse?' Tommy asked.

'It was one of his favourite tricks,' Nursie told her. 'There's a flowering bush called woad. He used to make blue dye out of the leaves.'

Reynard had made the yellow dye for

the sheets using leaves, Tommy recalled. Maybe he had got the idea from hearing about Sir Ferdy's trick.

At dinner that night, Tommy dipped her spoon into her soup cautiously, half expecting something terrible to happen. Then she remembered that she had no reason to worry. Reynard wouldn't be playing his tricks around the castle anymore.

'Reynard has been sent home,' she told Mrs Moon, who was rolling out pastry. 'He was the trickster.'

The cook shook her head and tutted. 'So I heard. It'll be a great disappointment to his family. He was the first Foxe in

generations to work at the castle. They
were so proud.'

'Reynard is a Foxe?' Tommy said. 'There's
a knight in the wall hanging in the great
hall called Sir Ferdinand Foxe.'

'That's right.' Mrs Moon wiped her
floury hands on her apron. 'Sir Ferdy was
… let me see … He was Reynard's great-
grandfather, I believe.'

So that's who the knight in the wall

hanging had reminded her of: Reynard!

'Poor silly lad,' Mrs Moon went on. 'He could have been a knight one day, but now he's got to walk all the way home to the farm in disgrace.'

'But why doesn't he ride his horse?' Tommy asked.

'His horse?' the cook retorted. 'Reynard doesn't have a horse. Where did you get a notion a like that?'

'The croco— I mean, someone said they saw him riding one.'

Mrs Moon snorted. 'Don't be silly, girl! A boy from a poor farming family isn't likely to have a horse of his own, is he?'

'I suppose not,' said Tommy slowly. But if it wasn't Reynard's horse, she wondered, whose horse was it?

CHAPTER 8

TOMMY SPENT THE NEXT MORNING in the bow chamber. She had a lot to learn about caring for the crossbows and longbows. As she was sharpening the steel tip of an arrow, she heard footsteps enter the armoury at a run.

She went to the doorway and saw two squires, one with fair hair and a big nose, the other with dark hair and goggly eyes.

'Have you seen him?' demanded the fair-haired squire.

Smith put down his hammer. 'Seen who?' he asked.

'Reynard,' said the squire with goggly eyes.

'Reynard was sent home yesterday,' said the smith. 'He's gone.'

'No he's not.' The first squire sounded excited. 'He's played another trick. Sir Benedict thinks he must be hiding somewhere in the castle and he's got all the squires searching for him.'

Tommy spoke up. 'What did he do?'

The dark-haired squire turned his goggly

gaze in her direction. 'Go to the stables and see for yourself.'

Tommy turned to Smith. 'Can I?'

At his nod, she set off for the stables.

In the yard, the stable master was shouting at a stable boy to fetch as much water as he could carry. 'Be quick about it!' he ordered.

'What's happened?' Tommy asked. 'Was it the bay stallion again?'

The stable master spun around. 'Oh, it's you, Sword Girl.' He sounded distracted. 'What's that about a bay stallion? I told you: there are no bay stallions in our stables. Oi! You there! What do you think you're laughing at?' He advanced on a pair of grooms who were laughing and pointing at something inside the stables.

Tommy felt a gentle nudge at her shoulder and turned to find Bess standing behind her. The chestnut mare's nostrils were flaring. 'It wasn't the bay, it was his master: the redhead. You should see what he's done to Belle.'

'Belle? Isn't that Lady Beatrix's horse?' Sir Walter's wife had a beautiful white mare, Tommy knew.

'That's right. Look!'

A stable boy was leading Belle into the yard. 'Oh!' Tommy exclaimed when she saw her. Lady Beatrix the Bored's white mare was blue!

Tommy stood staring at the blue horse, her hand to her mouth.

'What's wrong, Sword Girl?' asked Bess. 'You look like you've seen a ghost.'

'You say the person who dyed Belle blue had red hair?' Tommy said urgently.

'I saw him with my own eyes,' Bess responded angrily. 'And I told Sir Benedict, too.'

Was what she suspected even possible?

Tommy didn't know. But she had to find out …

Tommy found Lil down by the moat with the crocodiddle. 'Have you heard what happened to Belle?' she asked.

'I have,' said the cat. 'And I must say, I'm surprised that Reynard would dare to sneak back to the castle after Sir Benedict sent him away.'

'I don't think it was Reynard who played this trick,' Tommy said. 'Or any of the other tricks. Lil, do you believe in ghosts?'

'Of course,' said the cat. 'I see them around the castle all the time.'

'Me too,' said the crocodiddle.

'But if they're so common, why haven't I ever seen them?' asked Tommy, surprised.

'For some reason, people rarely do,' the cat replied. 'Animals must have better eyesight.'

'So when you saw Reynard riding a horse into the castle late at night, Mr

Crocodiddle, could that could have been a ghost?' said Tommy.

'It could have been, except that I recognised the red-haired boy.'

Tommy turned to Lil. 'And when the pigeon saw someone sprinkling itching powder on Sir Walter's sheets, could it have been a ghost he saw?' she asked.

'I suppose it could have been,' said the cat. 'But the pigeon was certain it was Reynard. Tommy, why are you asking about ghosts?'

'Because I believe Reynard is innocent,' declared Tommy. 'Quick – we have to find Sir Benedict.'

CHAPTER 9

THE KNIGHT WAS IN the great hall once again, seated by himself at the middle of the long table. He was looking very cross.

'I hope you've come to tell me you've found Reynard,' he said when he saw Tommy and Lil.

'No, sir,' said Tommy. 'We haven't. But, Sir Benedict, I know who has been playing all these tricks.'

'So do I,' said Sir Benedict. 'Enough witnesses have seen Reynard in the act.'

'No,' said Tommy. 'It's not Reynard, sir. I think ...' She hesitated. Would Sir Benedict believe her? 'I think the trickster is Sir Ferdinand Foxe.'

Sir Benedict stared at her in astonishment. 'Sir Ferdy?' he said. 'But, Tommy, Ferdy has been dead for a hundred years!'

'I know, sir,' Tommy said. 'But the tricks all started after I was woken in the night by a horse and rider. I thought it must be a messenger, but no one had seen him. At least, no *person* had seen him. But Bess said a new horse had arrived in the stables, and the crocodiddle recognised the rider; he thought it was Reynard.'

'That's impossible,' said Sir Benedict. 'Reynard doesn't have a horse.'

'No, but Sir Ferdinand did, and he was Reynard's great-grandfather – I saw him in the wall hanging over there.' She turned and pointed. 'He looks exactly like Reynard. And, Sir Benedict ...'

Sir Benedict finished the sentence for her. 'Sir Ferdy is riding a blue horse,' he said slowly. He added, 'I've always wondered about that.'

'Nursie says that Sir Ferdy was a well-known trickster, and dyeing horses blue was his favourite trick of all. And the trickster also dyed the sheets in the laundry yellow.'

Sir Benedict was looking thoughtful. 'So you're suggesting our trickster is the ghost of Sir Ferdy?'

'Yes, sir.'

'Hmm. It's going to be very difficult to prove this for sure if we can't see him.'

'*You* can't see him,' said Lil, 'but *we* can. And that's why all the witnesses have been birds and animals. Instead of squires searching the castle, it should be us.'

Sir Benedict tapped his finger on the table for a few seconds while he considered this. Finally, he pushed back his chair and stood up.

'You're right. Lil, I want you to take over the search. I'm going to ride to the Foxe family farm. If Reynard is there, I'll know for sure he's not our trickster.' He smiled wryly. 'And I'll have another apology to make.'

So when Sir Benedict had set off for the

Foxes' farm, the pigeon surveyed the castle from the air, the crocodiddle checked the grounds outside and Tommy accompanied Lil as she checked inside the castle walls. They began with the places where the trickster had been before, starting with the stables, then the laundry, then the kitchen.

They were in the pantry when Lil said, 'Oh, dear. Not replacing the salt with sugar again. You've already played that trick.'

Tommy heard someone say, 'Eeek!', though she couldn't see anyone else in the pantry.

'Who are you, girl, and how come you can see me?' asked a voice. Then: 'Oh, there's a cat. I always forget that animals have much better eyesight than humans.'

'We know all about you and your tricks, Sir Ferdy,' Lil said. 'You might as well show yourself.'

'If you insist,' the voice said, and as Tommy watched in amazement a short, stout, red-haired knight shimmered into view. 'But how did you know it was me?'

'You'll have to ask our Keeper of the

Blades,' Lil said, gesturing to Tommy with her paw.

The knight's eyes widened. 'The Keeper of the Blades is a girl? Things have certainly changed since my day.'

'She's the first,' Lil told him. 'And one day she'll be the first-ever girl knight.'

Tommy blushed. 'I hope so,' she said.

'Well if you worked out it was me playing those tricks, you must have a good head on your shoulders. Tell me how you did it.'

And so Tommy described again how she'd heard the mysterious rider in the night, all the way to realising that the trickster in the wall hanging was Reynard's great-grandfather.

'I have a great-grandson working at the castle?' asked the ghost, interested. 'I'd like to meet the lad.'

'That's a good idea,' said Lil. 'You can apologise for all the trouble you've caused him. He was sent away from the castle because of your tricks, but Sir Benedict should be bringing him back soon. Let's go wait in the bow chamber.'

Sir Ferdy faded from Tommy's view, and

the three of them walked across the great courtyard.

Smith wasn't in the armoury, but Reynard was, strutting around the room like he'd never been away.

'You're back already,' said Tommy.

'Sir Benedict came to fetch me home and apologised to me personally,' said Reynard. 'I suppose you'll be wanting to do the same, Sword Girl. I bet you feel pretty stupid for telling Sir Benedict I was the trickster when I wasn't.'

'I didn't tell—' Tommy began, then stopped. She had thought Reynard was the trickster. She supposed she did owe him an apology. 'I'm sorry,' she said. 'And there's someone else who wants to apologise to you too.'

'Who?' said Reynard rudely. 'Your stupid cat?' He aimed a kick at Lil, who dodged it nimbly, though she growled.

'No – the real trickster,' said Tommy as a red-haired knight appeared. 'Reynard, this is Sir Ferdinand Foxe. He's your great-grandfather.'

'My – my – *eeeeek!*' Reynard let out a terrified shriek and fled from the room.

Sir Ferdy shook his head. 'That's my great-grandson?' He sounded disappointed. 'Seems like a cowardy custard to me.' He looked around the armoury – at the fire glowing in the fireplace, at the stack of shields awaiting repair on Smith's bench, at the long rack of swords visible through the door to the sword chamber – then sighed. 'It's been wonderful to see dear old Flamant Castle again,' he said. 'But it's time for me to move on. Perhaps Roses Castle could use some haunting …'

'We'll see you off,' Tommy offered. She wanted to be sure that the trickster really did leave!

The ghost faded into thin air, then Tommy and Lil walked with him to the stables. Tommy couldn't see Sir Ferdy's bay stallion, but she could guess where he was from the indignant neighs coming from the horses' stalls.

Some minutes later she heard a softly called 'Goodbye', and a faint clatter of hooves.

'He's gone,' said Lil with satisfaction. 'Now things can get back to normal around here.'

When they returned to the armoury, they saw Sir Benedict standing in the doorway of the bow chamber. He turned and beckoned them over.

Reynard was sitting on his stool in the bow chamber, a large orange ring painted around each eye.

The physician was standing beside the Keeper of the Bows with a pot and

a brush. 'I found this poor lad out in the great courtyard screaming that he had seen a ghost. Of course, that's not possible. Clearly his eyes are playing tricks on him. Fortunately, I happen to know the cure for Trick Eye: carrot juice mixed with pigeon droppings.' He dabbed some more of the orange mixture on Reynard.

'It's not my eyes – she did it!' Reynard shouted, pointing at Tommy. 'She played a terrible trick on me.'

'Is this true, Tommy?' Sir Benedict asked. His voice was grave, but Tommy saw that his eyes were twinkling.

'I'm sorry, sir,' she said. 'But I promise there'll be no more tricks at Flamant Castle.'

The knight put a hand on her shoulder. 'You did well to find the trickster, Tommy,' he said quietly. 'Good work.' Then he raised his voice. 'Though there are some tricks that knights find very useful.'

Tommy looked at him uncertainly. 'There are?'

'Absolutely,' said the knight. 'Sword-fighting tricks! Bring Jasper out to the courtyard and I'll show you some.'

'Yes, sir!' said Tommy. Her heart felt as light as a feather as she hurried off to fetch her sword.

JOIN TOMMY AND
HER FRIENDS FOR ANOTHER
SWORD GIRL
ADVENTURE IN

Pigeon
PROBLEMS

CHAPTER 1

'Sir Walter ...'

Clang!

'In the great courtyard.'

Clang!

Tommy put the sword she was holding on the bench. 'Did you hear something, Lil?' she asked the black and white cat sitting on the stone floor of the sword chamber.

Lil, who had been polishing her whiskers

while Tommy polished swords, paused in her grooming. 'I thought I heard something about Sir Walter,' she said.

Tommy went to the doorway of the sword chamber and saw that a page had entered the armoury and was standing in front of the smith.

The ringing sound of hammer on metal ceased as Smith stilled his hand. 'What was that you said, lad?'

'Sir Walter the Bald wants everyone to gather in the great courtyard,' the boy announced.

Tommy and Lil exchanged looks. Why would Sir Walter the Bald, the nobleman who owned Flamant Castle, call everyone together?

'Do you know why, lad?' Clearly Smith was wondering the same thing.

'No, sir. Sir Benedict just asked me and the other pages to deliver the message to all corners of the castle.' And the boy darted off.

The smith laid down his hammer. 'That's mighty strange,' he muttered. 'And on Sir Benedict's orders, he says.' Sir Benedict was Flamant Castle's bravest knight.

'What is it, Smith?' Tommy asked. 'Do you think our enemies are attacking?' Her heart began to beat faster.

The smith shook his grizzled head. 'I don't know, Sword Girl. We'd best join the others in the courtyard and find out.' He raised his voice. 'Reynard?'

There was no answer from the bow chamber.

'Reynard!'

At last the Keeper of the Bows emerged from the bow chamber, yawning and rubbing his eyes.

'What is it?' the red-haired boy asked grumpily. 'I was busy.'

Tommy wasn't sure she believed him. It looked to her as if Reynard had been asleep.

'Sir Walter wants to see us,' the smith said.

Tommy could hear the murmur of voices as the courtyard outside the armoury began to fill with people. She was about to follow Smith and Reynard out the door when she realised she was still

holding the rag she used for polishing swords. She darted back into the sword chamber, Lil at her heels.

'What do you think is happening, Lil?' Tommy asked as she dropped the rag next to a pot of clove-scented oil.

'I haven't a clue,' said the cat. 'But it must be important. I can't remember the last time Sir Walter ordered everyone to gather like this.'

'What's important?' came a voice from the shadows. 'Tell me, dearie.'

Tommy glanced at the small rack of swords that stood in the room's darkest corner. When she had first become Flamant Castle's Keeper of the Blades, caring for all the bladed weapons in the armoury, she had been surprised to find a collection of dusty, neglected swords. Known as the Old Wrecks, these were swords that had never been carried into battle, and thus were never used by the knights. But Tommy had discovered that the swords were inhabited by the spirits of their previous owners. That the Old Wrecks could talk – and many of the castle's animals too – was a secret known only to her and Sir Benedict.

'Sir Walter has ordered everyone to the great courtyard,' Tommy told Nursie, the sabre that had spoken.

'Ooh, what could my little darling be up to?' Nursie wondered. 'It'll be a wonderful treat for you all, I'm sure.' Nursie had been Sir Walter's nursemaid when he was a boy, and she always referred to the nobleman as her 'little darling'.

'I wouldn't be so sure about that,' said a long-handled dagger in a deep voice. 'It sounds serious to me.'

'What would you know, Bevan Brumm?' the sabre demanded. 'You were a merchant. I'm sure I know more about the workings of the castle than you.'

Before the argument could go any further, Jasper Swann, a slender sword that had belonged to a squire close to Tommy's own age, said, 'You'd better go.'

Just then the smith called impatiently, 'Are you coming, Sword Girl?'

'I'll be back as soon as I can,' Tommy promised the Old Wrecks, then hurried out to join the throng.

ABOUT THE AUTHOR

FRANCES WATTS was born in the medieval city of Lausanne, in Switzerland, and moved to Australia when she was three. After studying literature at university she began working as an editor. Her bestselling picture books include *Kisses for Daddy* and the 2008 Children's Book Council of Australia award-winner, *Parsley Rabbit's Book about Books* (both illustrated by David Legge). In 2012 she won the Prime Minister's Literary Award for Children's Fiction for *Goodnight, Mice!* (illustrated by Judy Watson). Frances is also the author of a series about two very unlikely superheroes, Extraordinary Ernie and Marvellous Maud, and the highly acclaimed children's fantasy/adventure series, the Gerander Trilogy.

Frances lives in Sydney's inner west, and divides her time between writing and editing. Her cat doesn't talk.

ABOUT THE ILLUSTRATOR

GREGORY ROGERS has always loved art and drawing so it's no surprise he became an illustrator. He was the first Australian to win the prestigious Kate Greenaway Medal. The first of his popular wordless picture book series, *The Boy, the Bear, the Baron, the Bard*, was selected as one of the Ten Best Illustrated Picture Books of 2004 by the *New York Times* and short-listed for the Children's Book Council of Australia Book of the Year Award in 2005. The third book, *The Hero of Little Street*, won the CBCA Picture Book of the Year in 2010. Gregory loves movies and music, and is a collector of books, antiques and anything odd and unusual.

He lives in Brisbane above a bookshop cafe with his cat Sybil.

For Every
Individual...

Renew by Phone
269-5222

Renew on the Web
www.indypl.org

For General Library Information
please call 275-4100